THREE UNOFFICIAL ADVENTURES FOR MINECRAFTERS!

THE GIGANTIC BOOK OF GRAPHIC NOVELS FOR MINECRAFTERS

CARA J. STEVENS
ART BY WALKER MELBY AND FRED BORCHERDT

SKY PONY PRESS
NEW YORK

Copyright © 2019 by Hollan Publishing, Inc.

Minecraft® is a registered trademark of Notch Development AB.

The Minecraft game is copyright © Mojang AB.

Sky Pony Press books may be purchased in bulk at special discounts for sales promotion, corporate gifts, fund-raising, or educational purposes. Special editions can also be created to specifications. For details, contact the Special Sales Department, Sky Pony Press, 307 West 36th Street, 11th Floor, New York, NY 10018 or info@skyhorsepublishing.com.

Sky Pony® is a registered trademark of Skyhorse Publishing, Inc.®, a Delaware corporation.

Minecraft® is a registered trademark of Notch Development AB. The Minecraft game is copyright © Mojang AB.

Visit our website at www.skyponypress.com.

10 9 8 7 6 5 4 3 2 1

Library of Congress Cataloging-in-Publication Data is available on file.

Cover design by Brian Peterson
Cover illustration by Fred Borcherdt and Walker Melby

Print ISBN: 978-1-5107-4047-1
Ebook ISBN: 978-1-5107-4238-3

Printed in China

AN UNOFFICIAL GRAPHIC NOVEL
FOR MINECRAFTERS

REDSTONE JUNIOR HIGH

ZOMBIES ATE MY HOMEWORK

BOOK 1

CARA J. STEVENS

ART BY FRED BORCHERDT

SKY PONY PRESS
NEW YORK

PIXEL: A girl with an unusual way with animals and other creatures

SKY: Pixel's first friend at Redstone Junior High

UMA: A mysterious, quiet girl who lurks in the shadows

CHARACTERS

ROB: A surprisingly friendly zombie

TINA AND THE VIOLETS: Pixel's sassy downstairs neighbor and her sidekicks

PRINCIPAL REDSTONE: The head of Redstone Junior High

INTRODUCTION

If you have played Minecraft, then you know all about Minecraft worlds. They're made of blocks you can mine, creatures you can interact with, and lands you can visit. On the outer edges of one world is an ordinary farm with ordinary animals, ordinary people, and one extraordinary girl.

The girl's name is Pixel and when our story begins, Pixel has no idea that she is destined for greatness, or even destined to be noticed by anyone other than her animal friends. The youngest of twelve brothers and sisters, Pixel has always kept to herself, preferring the company of animals and neutral mobs to other miners.

We join Pixel the day before she is set to embark on the biggest journey of her life. She is heading to the prestigious Redstone Junior High, a school for gifted students, where no hostile mob has dared enter for more than one hundred years. That is about to change.

CHAPTER 1

LEAVING HOME

You have to come back...

That's ALL you got after all this time out here?

Shoo! Why are these animals always following you?

I understand them and they understand me.

My guess is that they figured out you're a walking snack machine.

Why do I have to come back? I'm not done picking mushrooms like you asked me to.

NOM, NOM

MUNCH

Hey!

CLATTER

CRUNCH

I'll miss everyone for sure...

Bye! Thanks for dinner! See ya! Let' play checkers!

...But I've always dreamed that there's another place for me. A place where I fit in better than I do here.

Mom? Dad? I'd like to go.

I though you would. already pac your bags, in case.

We'll miss you so much, young lady.

Be good and pay attention. We expe you to represent ou family well and to m us as proud as you always do.

Thanks, you guys! I'll n you, too. And I promise t make you proud!

I can't sleep. Maybe I'll just go check on the animals and say goodbye. I won't have a chance in the morning.

What's wrong, Lola? It's just me. Don't be scared!

Aaaah! A horde of spiders! And they look mean!

I'd better light a torch.

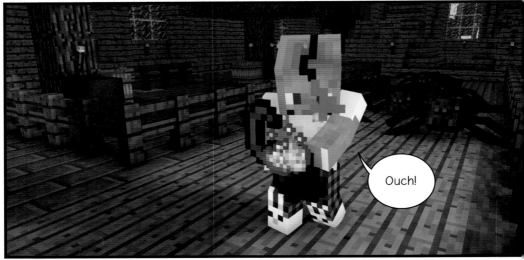

Ouch!

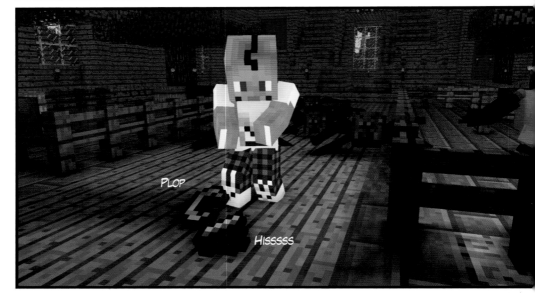

PLOP

Hisssss

CHAPTER 2

NEW

BEGINNINGS

How many roommates do I have?

None. It's just you.

All to myself? Really? I share with my five sisters at home.

We're sorry about the room. We never use it, but I think you'll make good use of it.

I hope so...

We just got here. How does everyone seem to know each other already?

Attention, all students. Report to the dining hall for a welcome lecture.

I guess unpacking will have to wait.

Um...hi. I'm Pixel.

It's not a big deal. I've been doing it all my life.

That's really cool. I can't speak to animals. I just make stuff.

Doesn't make it less cool.

Please don't tell anyone!

It'll be our secret.

What's this arrow for?

Ouch! Why did you do that?

Sorry. Hold still. It's tipped so we can sneak back in without Principal Redstone catching us.

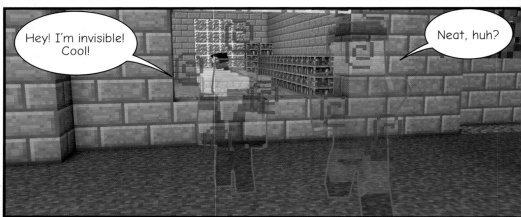

Hey! I'm invisible! Cool!

Neat, huh?

I'm Sky, by the way.

I'm Pixel. Nice to meet you.

You're the first person I've met here who is actually nice.

Same here. But I've only met three people so far.

Now you've met four.

CHAPTER 3

HUNGRY
ZOMBIES

Read chapter 1 for a refresher on command block placement. I'm going to check on a trap I set to see if it's working. I'll be back in a few minutes.

Come with me to test my science project.

But we're supposed to be studying.

I know this stuff already. I figured it out in kindergarten.

I don't know it at all.

I'll walk you through it now if you'll come with me tonight to try out my project. Deal?

Deal!

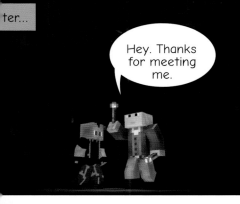

You've probably never been face-to-face with a hostile mob. If you had, you'd be scared.

Right, that's why I'm not scared.

Wow! Is that your trap? Have you tried it out yet?

Not yet. We need a hostile mob to test it on.

You're not going to hurt anyone with this, are you?

RUSTLE

I hope not. I wish I could get a willing subject.

What if I could find you someone...

Z-zzzombie!

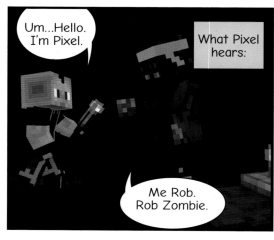

Um...Hello. I'm Pixel.

What Pixel hears:

Me Rob. Rob Zombie.

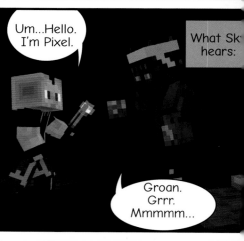

Um...Hello. I'm Pixel.

What Sk hears:

Groan. Grrr. Mmmmm...

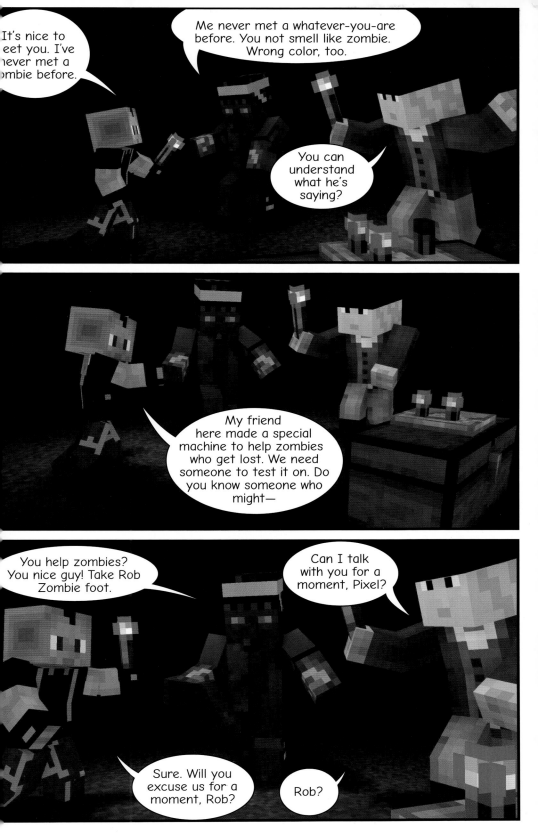

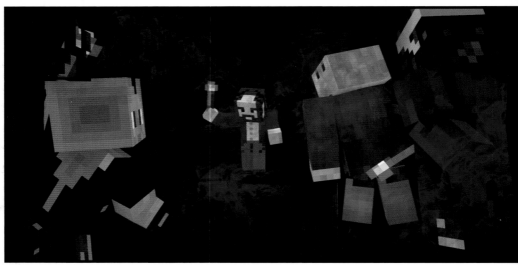

PLUNK!

I know there are students out here hiding. It's not safe here at night. You won't get in trouble if you show yourselves now.

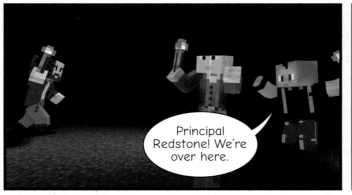

I've heard about your device and I'm very impressed, but you now it's dangerous out ere. It smells like a zombie attack is afoot.

A foot?

Not an actual foot. There are no zombie feet just lying around...

"Afoot" is an old-fashioned way of saying something's happening right now. Glad I could make this a learning experience for you.

Now back to bed with you both. I'll let your mistake slide this time, but no more sneaking out at night.

CHAPTER 4

SATURDAY IS
COMING

BEWARE OF
SATURDAY

I think all mobs can be scary if we don't understand them. Wouldn't it be great if we could get along instead of hurting each other?

That Night

KNOCK. KNOCK.

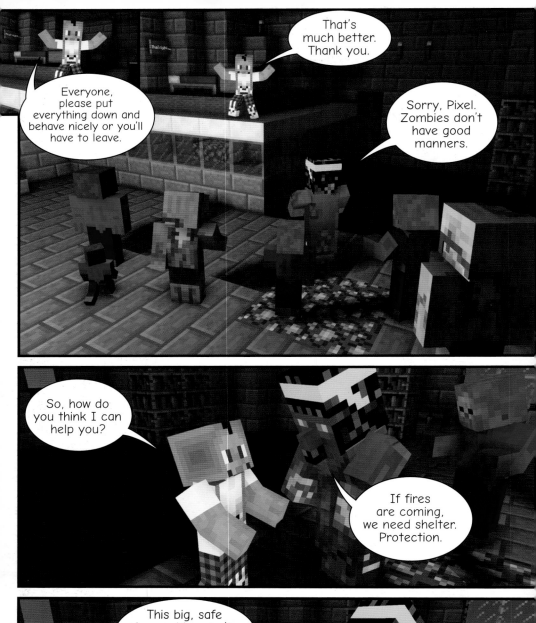

That's much better. Thank you.

Everyone, please put everything down and behave nicely or you'll have to leave.

Sorry, Pixel. Zombies don't have good manners.

So, how do you think I can help you?

If fires are coming, we need shelter. Protection.

This big, safe house. You won't even notice zombies are here.

No way! I'm sorry, but there is totally no way I can invite you guys in to stay here. No one can even know I can speak with you.

Zombies no like miners either. You only nice miner. You and boy with funny hat.

Remember... me loaned you foot, after all.

I understand. It's just that...

I'm not agreeing to shelter you guys, but I will ask Sky to help us figure out a way to fight fire with fire...

No fire! Zombies no fight with fire.

Sigh. It's just an expression, Rob. I'll ask him to help me p you find a way to n against whoever s trying to hurt u on Saturday.

BAM!   BAAK!

CHAPTER 5

STINKY NIGHT

Oh, excuse me.

Contraptions 101 will be the most important class you'll take this year...and maybe even your whole time here at Redstone Junior High.

I can't seem to stay awake today.

For our first project on mob containment, we'll break into teams.

What happened to you?

Out partying with zombies again?

Ha ha. Very funny. My upstairs neighbor decided to redecorate her room at midnight. I didn't get a wink of sleep last night. At least she looks more tired than I do.

Pixel! Stay awake!

CONTRAPTIONS 101 MR. QUARTZ

Be my partner on this project?

Sure. What project?

Mob containment. We're practically done with the trap anyway.

I didn't contribute anything yet.

You helped with the you-know-what testing. I couldn't have done that without you. Besides, we'll do the write-up together.

I can do that. I'm a pretty good writer-upper.

Writer-upper? That doesn't sound right...

I want to see drawings of your plan tomorrow, and you can't copy the spike trap I have on the board. That's mine.

CONTRAPTIONS 101 MR. QUARTZ

I really don't like this class. I learned this stuff ages ago!

I don't like it, either. It gives me the creeps.

They're not fooling anyone by calling it containment. All this talk is about "trapping" mobs when what they're really doing is killing them.

It's not even a good trap. You'd lose half your drops or more, depending on the mob.

Oh, excuse me.

Let go!

Pixel, it's me! What happened to you?

Bad night's sleep and a bad day to follow.

What happened? Zombies invade your bedroom last night?

Why would you say that?

It's just something my mom always says when I can't sleep at night. It's kind of creepy, actually, come to think of it. Why...did they?

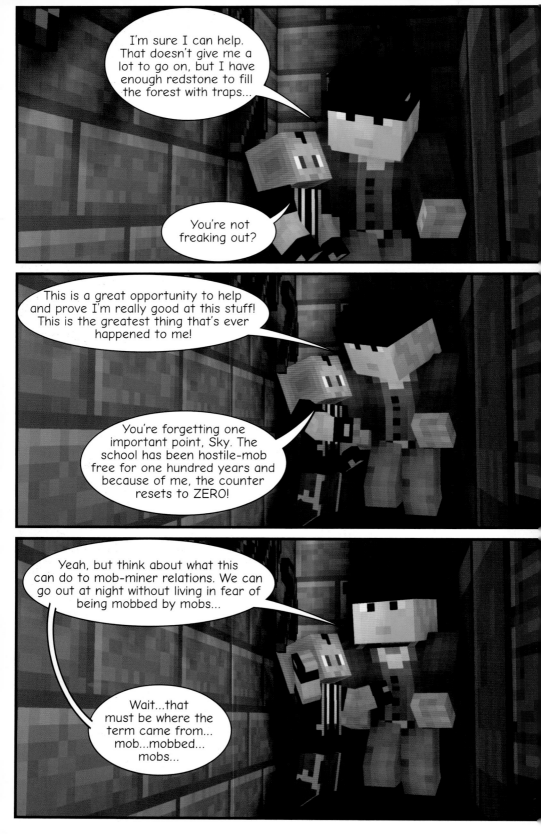

Come quickly. This way. Quietly, now. Don't let anyone see or hear you.

SHUFFLE. SHUFFLE.

GROAN.

SHHH!

We can't go to my room. Last night's close call was too close.

CHAPTER 6

SECRETS
REVEALED

...had a feeling you'd find each other.

You knew the zombies would find me?

I was hoping they would.

We have been observing you for some time for a unique ability. We thought you may not know about it yet but...

Um, I kind of figured it out already.

Of course. I see.

Zombies are not a very well-behaved bunch, are they?

They are just hungry, sir. I can ask them to behave.

So it's true, then. You can actually communicate with them directly?

Yes. I discovered it yesterday when you found us in the forest.

Oh, so that was the smell.

Sorry. We be quiet, Pixel!

Excuse me, but can you please quiet down? I'll give you more paper if you just cooperate and stay quiet.

What Principal Redstone hears.

Groan. Mmm.

Principal Redstone, this is my friend Rob. He came to us asking for help.

Friends and family are disappearing. Someone is making big fire and taking them away. Me no think we are safe.

I'm sorry, but I didn't get a word of that. It all sounded like moans and grunts to me.

Rob's family told him that someone has set fire to the other side of the forest and is driving out all the mobs and relocating them. It doesn't sound safe...or nice.

That is disturbing. And it confirms what I have heard from other miners around the area.

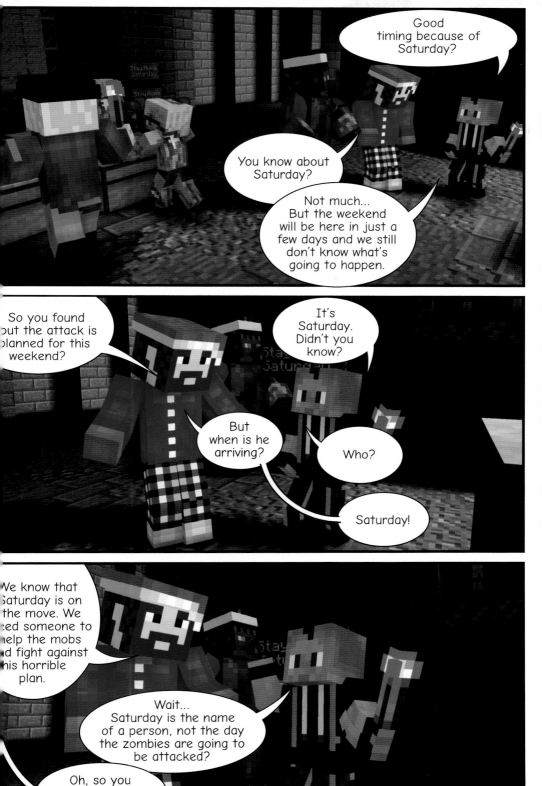

Saturday is a member of the SAMD, the Society for Advanced Mob Domestication. They pretend to be good guys, but make no mistake...they are not. They want to kill the mobs and use them for their drops. I've heard their real slogan is, "The only good z-o-m-b-i-e is a dead z-o-m-b-i-e."

That's horrible. Wait, why did you spell out the word zombie? They can't understand you.

Sorry. I forgot. And yes, it is horrible!

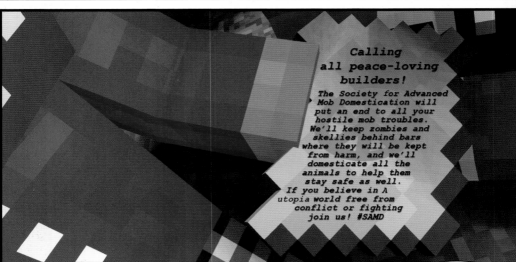

Calling all peace-loving builders!

The Society for Advanced Mob Domestication will put an end to all your hostile mob troubles. We'll keep zombies and skellies behind bars where they will be kept from harm, and we'll domesticate all the animals to help them stay safe as well. If you believe in A utopia world free from conflict or fighting join us! #SAMD

Here Rob. Take some fliers for you and some for your family. Or eat the blank paper. Pape with writing is importan We need it, okay?

Rob understand perfectly. Eat blank paper only. Gotcha, boss.

Saturday is a person?

You're both [ri]ght. We thought he was [a] when, not a who. But now [I] don't know when he's going [to] attack, and when he does, we [kno]w he isn't going to be nice or friendly.

You all keep doing the good work, but what we do here is super-duper top secret. No one can know what you're doing, and if they find out, no one can know I am involved.

Pixel, someone's coming!

CREAK!

How much do you want to bet I'm gonna find Pixel in here making all that noise...?

AAAAAAHHHH!

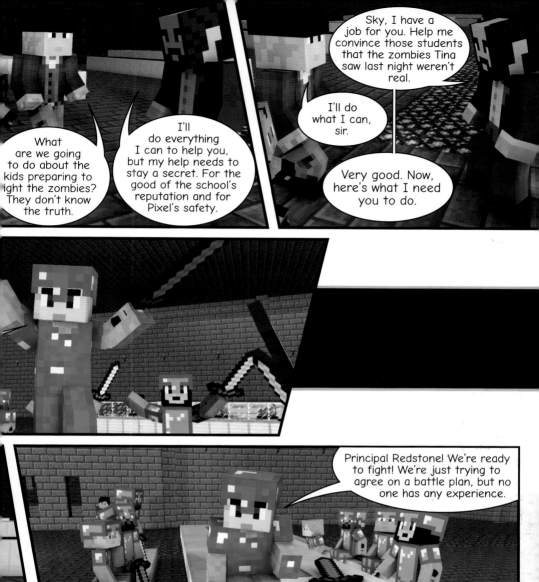

Sky, I have a job for you. Help me convince those students that the zombies Tina saw last night weren't real.

I'll do what I can, sir.

Very good. Now, here's what I need you to do.

What are we going to do about the kids preparing to fight the zombies? They don't know the truth.

I'll do everything I can to help you, but my help needs to stay a secret. For the good of the school's reputation and for Pixel's safety.

Principal Redstone! We're ready to fight! We're just trying to agree on a battle plan, but no one has any experience.

Sky has been secretly building a fake zombie army to help us with our training.

Grrunxx

That's not what I saw last night! There were real zombies. Lots of them. They were escaping through a window and no one was stopping them!

I don't ink it's that well esigned. It's not onvincing at all.

This is the worst fake zombie I've ever seen!

I don't think they're buying it, sir.

I think I should tell them the truth about me. It may be the only way to save the zombies.

If you're sure...But let's keep the element of danger and the news about Saturday out of this.

CHAPTER 7

THE ZOMBIE
STUDENT
ALLIANCE

The zombies came to me because they are being taken from their homes and destroyed. They mean us no harm.

If you want this to be a conversation instead of a dangerous battle, put your weapons down here and I'll tell you what I know.

And if you want to save yourselves from being attacked by zombies and having your brains eaten while you sleep, join me!

This should be interesting.

No, we ignore them and help the zombies.

Distraction.

A few people in our group can distract them, so they focus their energy on us while we go off in small groups and help those who need our help.

Yeah, but it taught us all a valuable lesson. I learned everything I could about self-defense, traps, and redstone. I got so good at it, I was recruited to come here. Serves that guy right. All he got was my rusty pickaxe and a couple of potions off me, but I have a bright new future. One that involves helping people and meeting all you guys.

Sounds e you should in charge of the raction crew. What you need to make this happen?

I don't know what you're up to, but it sounds messy and smelly.

feathers raw fish ink sacs sand slime

Exactly.

Good. The smellier, the better.

You're with me, Uma, if that's okay with you?

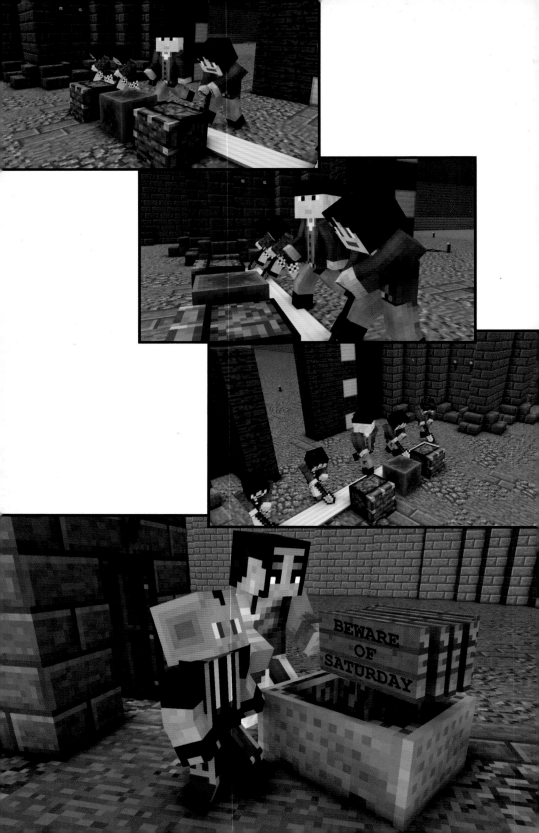

BEWARE
OF
SATURDAY

CHAPTER 8

SLIMED AND
FEATHERED

Get back here! Now you've really done it! You're all going to get kicked out now.

CRACK!

Oh, no.

I didn't do a thing. You stepped on the pressure plate.

That will be enough, children.

Tina, you and your friends go hit the showers. Use extra soap. In fact, shower twice.

And as for you, Sky, I'm assuming that was your idea of a distraction?

Yes, sir. Sorry about the mess.

But you'll all have to spend the rest of the day cleaning it up.

Now, Pixel...

Work it girls!

Keep going!

Three cheers for extra credit!

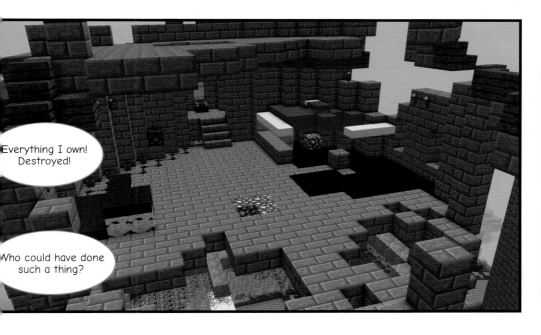

CHAPTER 9

BEST FRIENDS

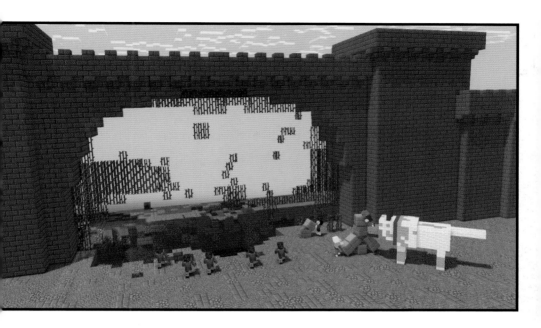

Hey, I'm no griefer. I love this school. My parents went here. My GRANDPARENTS went here. I've been looking forward to being at Redstane Junior High my whole life. I would never do anything to hurt it.

That's why it needs defending from people like you. It was mob-free for one hundred years. You're here for like a day and suddenly our halls are crawling with zombies and creepers are blowing themselves up at the gates. You do the math, Pixel.

Oh.

We understand, Tina. We are as concerned as you are, but I know Pixel is not at fault here.

She invited the zombies for a conference last night.

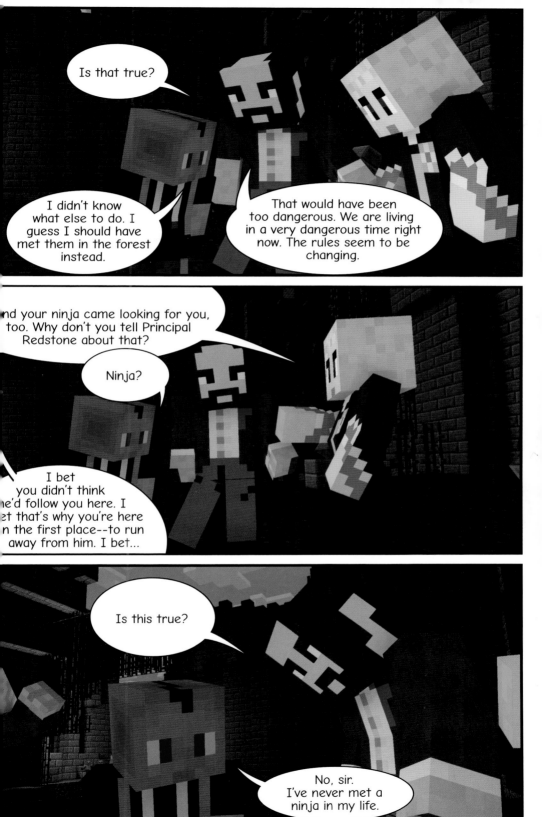

Tell me more about this ninja, Tina.

I was walking back to my room to shower off the fish and feathers when this guy just appeared in front of me

He asked me where Pixel lived and if I wanted to get her back. I said no, I could fight my own fights and didn't need a weirdo like him to help me, so he stormed off, mumbling he'd take care of her on his own.

How disturbing! Why didn't you tell me?

Because you're on Pixel's side. And maybe because I wanted to see what he would do.

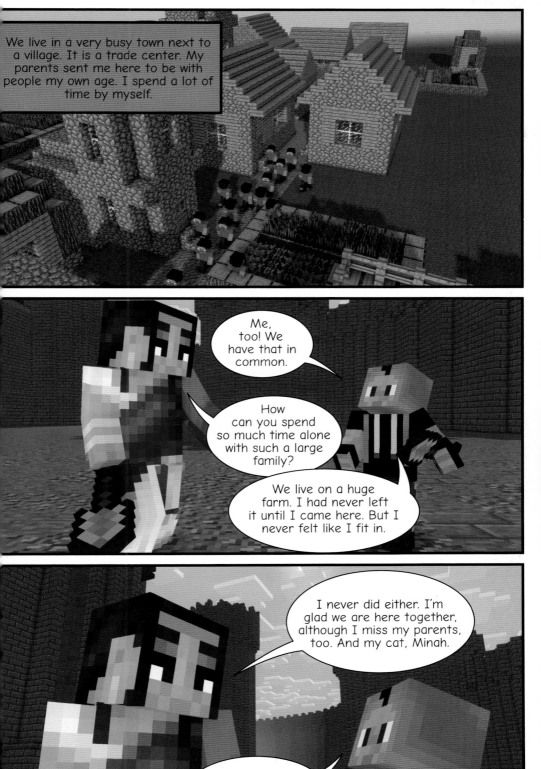

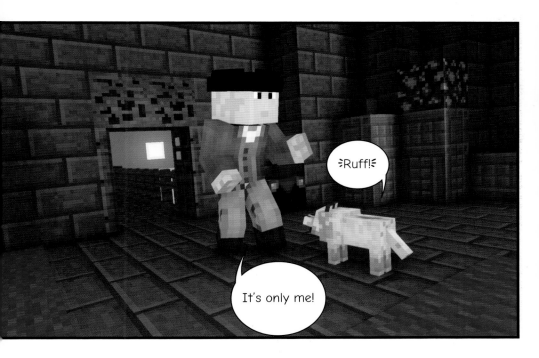

The new security system is in place, so Saturday can't come back without being detected...even if he is a real ninja. I checked in with the Zombie Alliance on my way here. They will be ready when we are. They took your knitting pattern and started making nets for the zombies to use for protection.

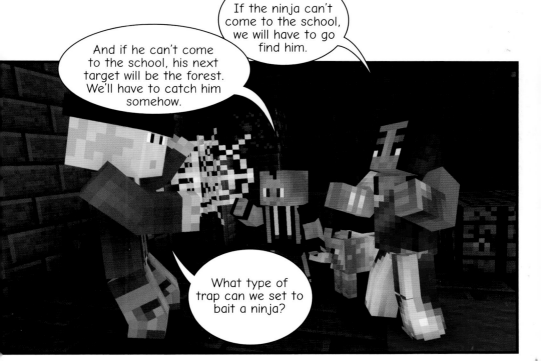

If the ninja can't come to the school, we will have to go find him.

And if he can't come to the school, his next target will be the forest. We'll have to catch him somehow.

What type of trap can we set to bait a ninja?

CHAPTER 10

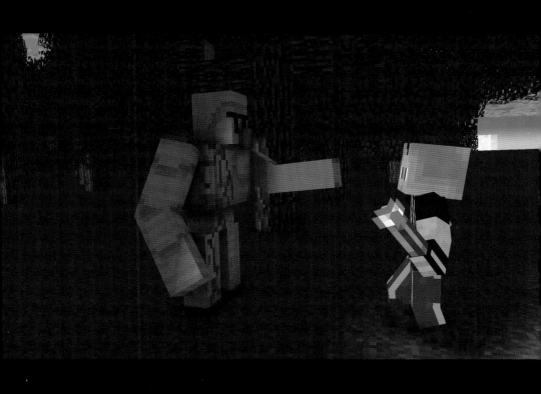

ATTACK OF
THE GOLEM

Hello? Rob? We're here. We need to talk to you!

Sprinkles? Where are you going?

That's weird. I thought for sure she was feeling protective of us, but then she just ran off.

They are uncertain. I think they want to know what they can do for us.

Maybe if we send them to look for more mobs, they can brin them back and can all meet here.

Maybe the wolves can track them down.

⸘Sniff. Sniff.⸘

I think they like that idea. We'll see if it works!

What's this?

They're nets. To throw over anyone who is attacking you. So you can protect yourselves.

Thank you. Good idea. Not safe here. You keep some nets too.

There. Take a look.

ee: If we fill the pit with slime, he won't be able to climb out nd he'll need us to rescue him before he loses all his health from bumping into them.

That's a great idea! I can totally make this happen. We have to figure out where to put it and how to get the ninja to the pit.

SHUFFLE. GRUNT. GROAN. MMM.

CHAPTER 11

NINJA
NO MORE

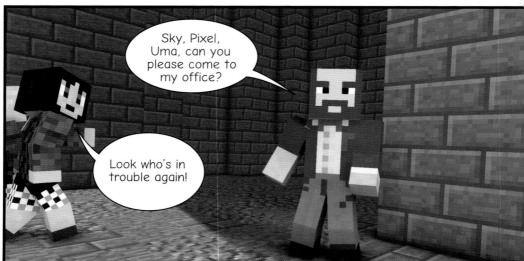

You three have a big night ahead of you. Why don't you go get some sleep? I'll tell everyone you're working on a special project.

Thanks, Principal Redstone. We've been up all night.

We could really use a nap!

Good luck tonight!

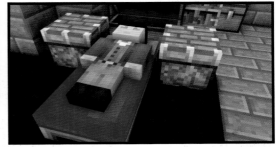

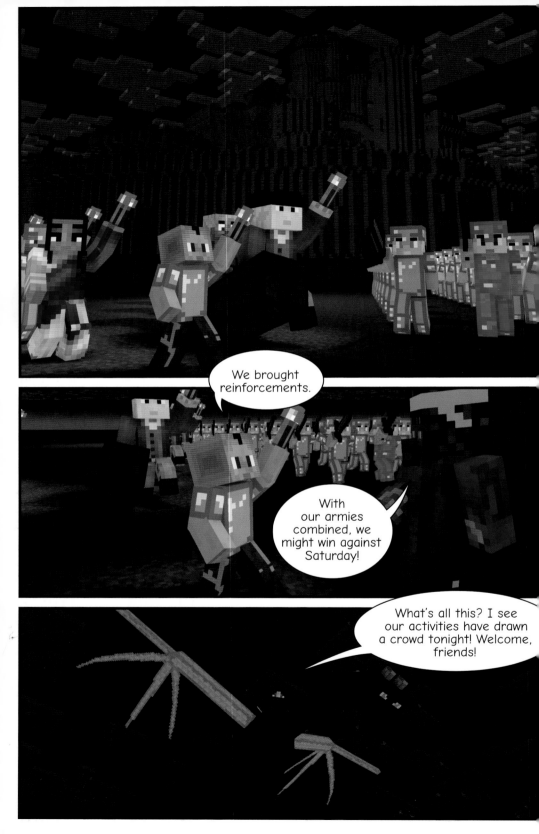

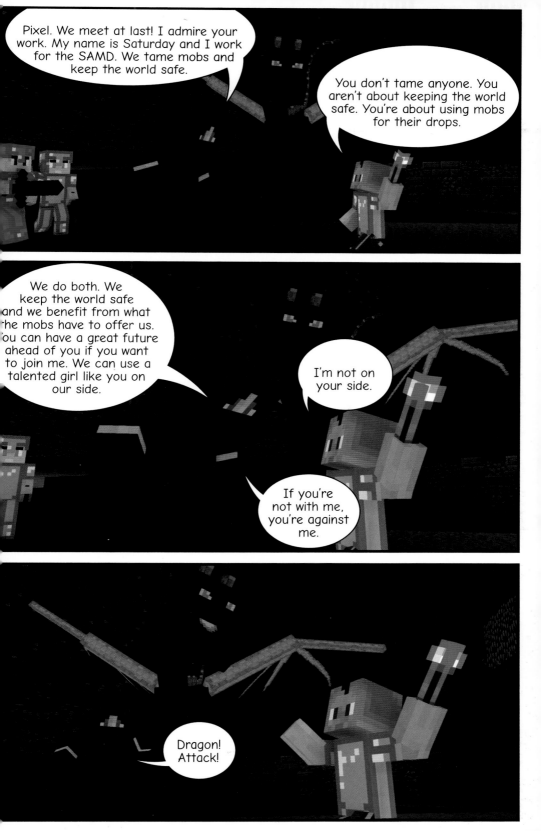

CHAPTER 12

JUST THE BEGINNING

I see your plans were successful. Well, done, you three.

Actually, it took all of us, sir. Tina and her friends protected us and the school, and we all lured Saturday out into the open.

But Pixel really saved the day when she worked her weird magic on the mobs.

Careful, Tina. That almost sounded like a compliment.

You earned it this time, even if it was your fault the zombies invaded in the first place.

We have captured Saturday. You'll find him at the edge of the forest.

Okay, who's with me? Let's go fix Pixel's room.

rs and counting

Hello. Are you Pixel's new friends?

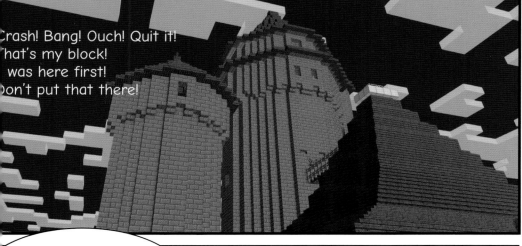

AN UNOFFICIAL GRAPHIC NOVEL
FOR MINECRAFTERS

REDSTONE JUNIOR HIGH

CREEPERS CRASHED MY PARTY

BOOK 2

CARA J. STEVENS

ART BY WALKER MELBY

SKY PONY PRESS
New York

PIXEL: A girl with an unusual way with animals and other creatures

SKY: A redstone expert who is also one of Pixel's best friends at school.

UMA: A fellow student at Redstone Junior High who can sense how people and mobs are feeling.

CHARACTERS

MR. Z: A teacher with a dark past.

TINA AND THE VIOLETS: Pixel's sassy downstairs neighbor and her sidekicks, who are more than they appear to be.

PRINCIPAL REDSTONE: The head of Redstone Junior High

SPRINKLES: A puppy who is fiercely loyal to Pixel, Sky, and Uma.

INTRODUCTION

If you have played Minecraft, then you know all about Minecraft worlds. They're made of blocks you can mine, creatures you can interact with, and lands you can visit. Deep in the heart of one of these worlds is an extraordinary school with students who have been handpicked from across the landscape for their unique abilities.

The school is Redstone Junior High. When we last left off in our story, Pixel and her friends, Uma and Sky, have defeated the evil Saturday, agent of the SAMD, an organization which seeks to enslave and destroy hostile mobs while claiming to protect them. The school has survived a zombie invasion, creeper explosions, swarms of hostile mobs and even a visit from the Ender Dragon, but these invasions remain a secret from the outside world.

As our story begins, things are just starting to get back to normal at school. Classes are in session and the students are eager to put their past adventures behind them and learn all about the mysteries of redstone contraptions and advanced building skills.

While Pixel and her friends want to make friends with the mobs, the memory of the zombie and creeper invasion is still fresh in many people's minds. We can feel the tension mounting between two groups of students, but there is another tension mounting outside the gates, too. One that could destroy the school and mob-miner relations across the world.

CHAPTER 1

A FRESH
START

Look out!

Hey, watch it!

You know there's no parkour allowed in the cafeteria, Sky. I'm telling Principal Redstone!

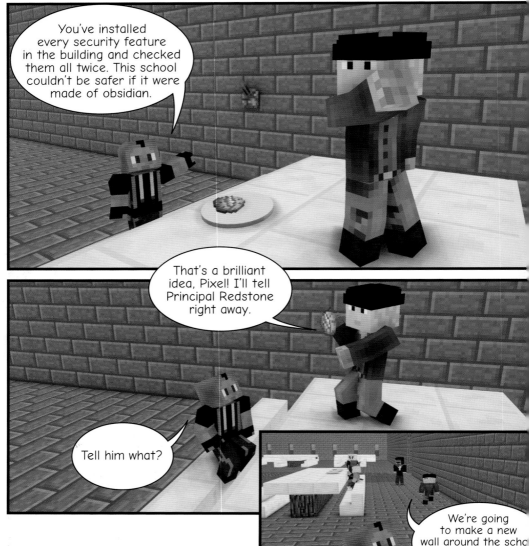

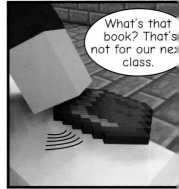

What are Pixel and her doofus friends up to now?

Hey! I think they have a pet dog. They're not allowed to have a pet dog. I'm going to tell the principal...

Go get it, Sprinkles!

She's such a cute puppy!

She is a very happy puppy, too. I believe playing fetch is her favorite game.

I wish I could sense things like you do, Uma. Or know what mobs are saying like you, Pixel.

Uma and I were born with those skills, Sky. But you've earned everything you know. You work so hard and that's why you know so much about contraptions.

It took all three of us and our skills to defeat that ninja, Saturday.

I'm glad all the zombies have been healed.

It's great that the zombies and skeletons are free now, but the forest looks so sad and burnt.

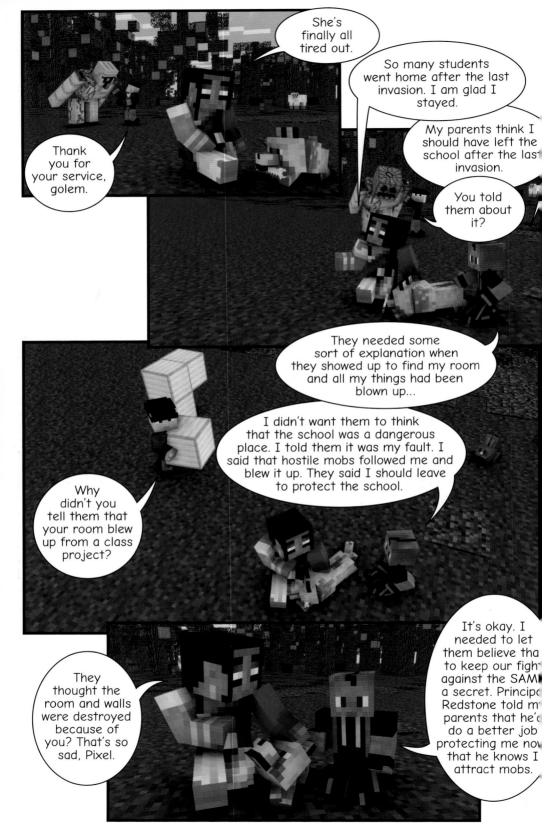

It's hard keeping a secret from my family, but having you two on my side really helps!

The danger isn't over just because Saturday has been defeated. Principal Redstone believes he was just one ninja warrior out of an entire army that wants to turn hostile mobs into slaves or destroy them.

The SAMD say they want to tame mobs and keep the world safe, but really they want to use them, and even kill them for drops like food and resources.

Principal Redstone is really worried that they will return and do terrible things to you and the mobs, not to mention the school and its reputation.

Oh!

Maybe I should have left.

I could go off and find the SAMD — whoever they are — and keep them away from the school.

Being here may be putting everyone and the school in danger.

Uma and I are a part of this, too. Uma can sense when there's evil or danger nearby, and I can do my best to protect us.

I only know when really hostile mobs are nearby or feel if someone is hurt or in trouble. I wish I could sense whether SAMD agents are lurking in the shadows, but my radar doesn't cover ninjas.

CHAPTER 2

ONCE UPON A TIME

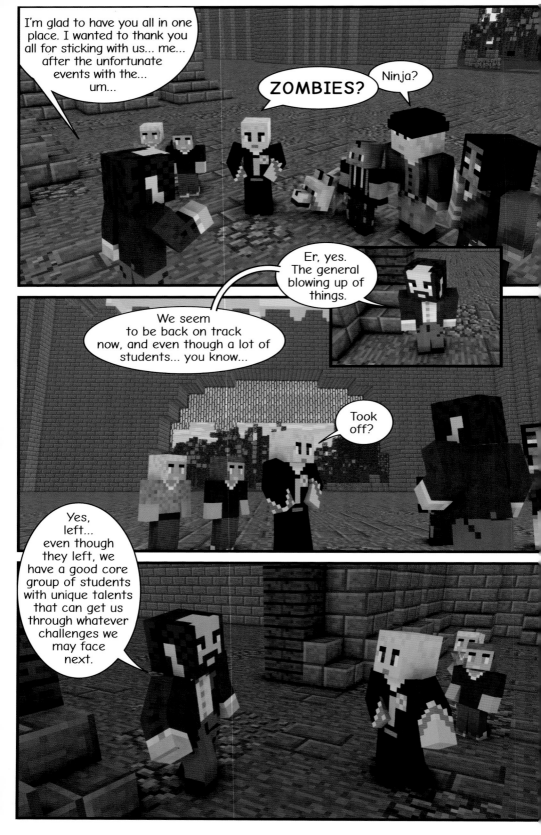

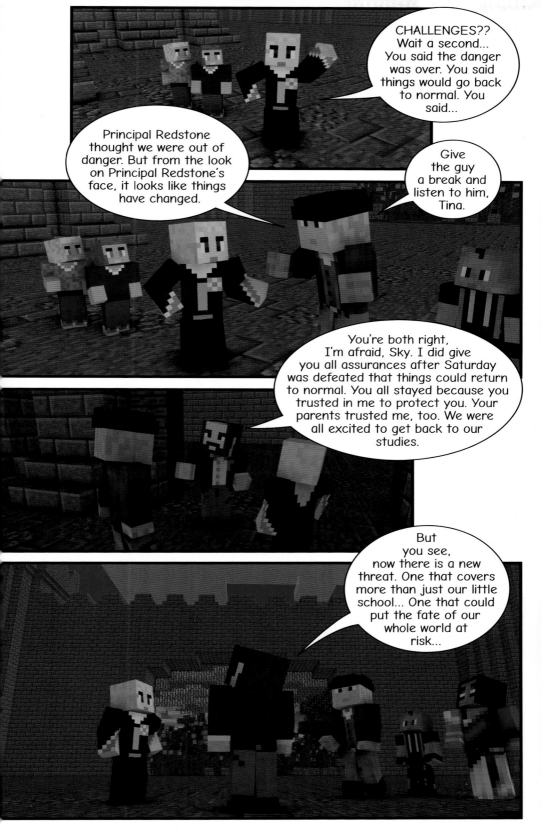

Long, long ago, the Overworld, the Nether, and the End wer[e] one. All villagers, miners, and mobs lived together in peac[e]

No one was hostile, and there was no need for weapons.

But one miner grew greedy and suspicious.

He turned the villagers and the miners against any mob that had the power to harm them. He said they were too dangerous, and should be banished from the Overworld.

There was a great war, and many died.

Hate built up and the world split ap[art]
separating the miners and villager[s]
from the other beings.

Time went on, and portals opened up
between the two worlds.

The "hostiles" came to the surface und[er]
the cover of darkness to get revenge [on]
the Overworld.

...ners and villagers discovered these portals and were able to travel down to the other worlds.

The universe was slowly knitting together, but the hatred stayed and fueled the divide among the creatures.

Some became purely hostile, like most zombies, guardians, and skeletons.

Others, like zombie pigmen, spiders, and Enderman
all stayed neutral unless their space was invaded.

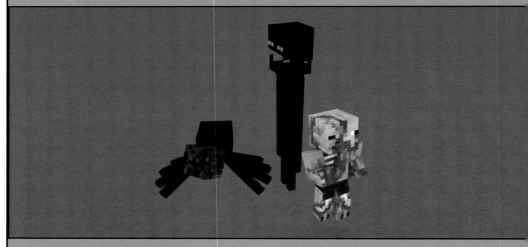

The situation proved to be too much for the sensitive creepers,
who shook and exploded at the mere sight of miners.

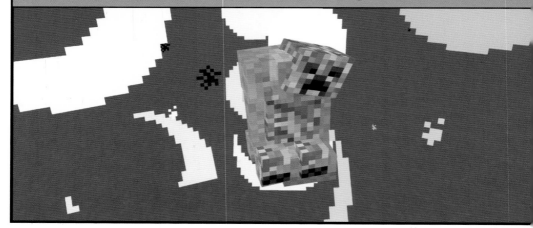

at brings us to today. Pixel is a new generation of miner who communicate across all mobs. Her powers give her the ability lessen the bond of hate among the different creatures and bring them together.

For all we know, there may be more people like her who can communicate in different ways.

Yes, Violet?

I'm afraid not.

Your story is amazing, but it sounds like with Saturday gone, the danger is past. Is it?

CHAPTER 3

A CHALLENGE

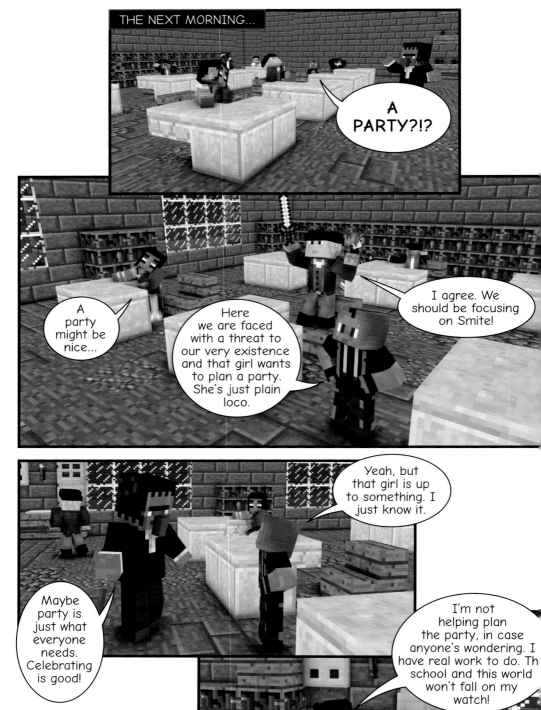

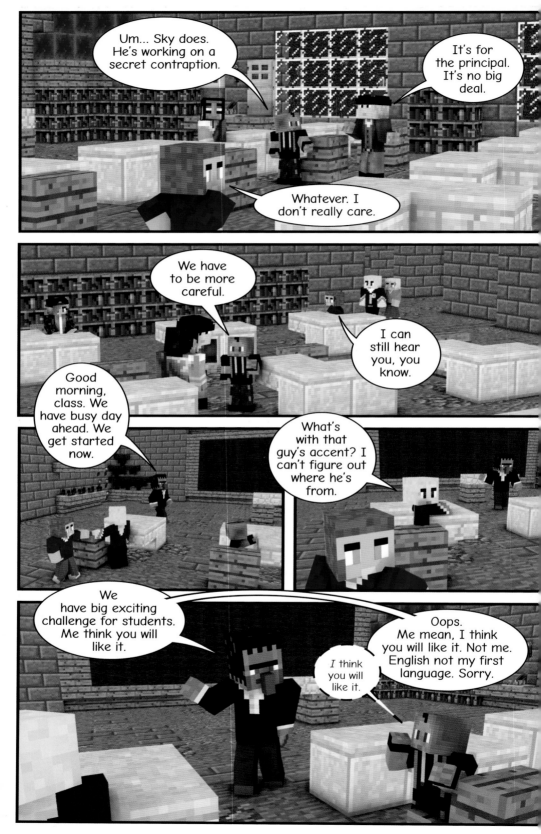

When do the challenges start?

Right NOW!

CHAPTER 4

CHALLENGE ACCEPTED

I'm next! I'll go!

Tina! No! Wait!

ZING!

DING!

Uma! Look out!

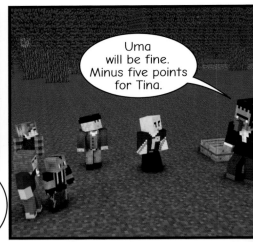

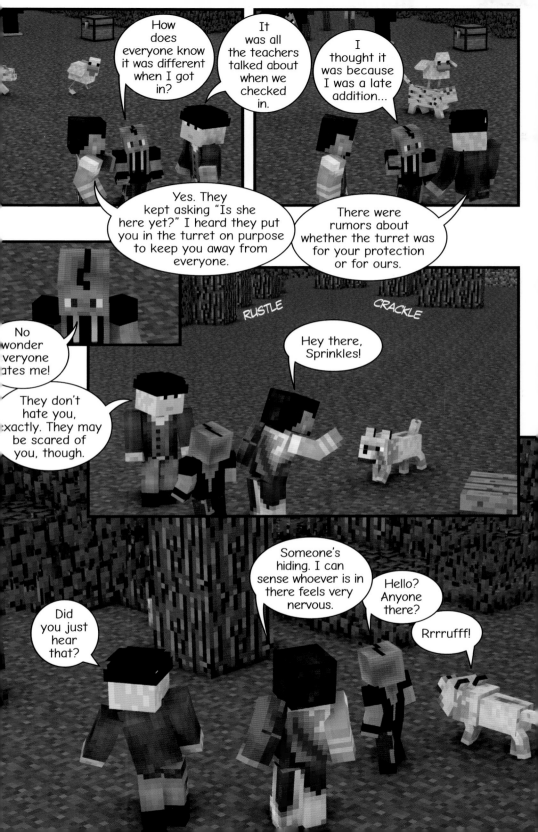

CHAPTER 5

SECRETS

Next we do enchanting challenge.

ENCHANT ELYTRA
What enchantments can you dream up for your wings to help you glide to victory?

Helmet
Mob Head
Elytra
Leggings

Okay, Teenie. You be captain. Pixie, you other captain.

Yes!

Captains pick teams. Teenie first.

My name is Tina. T-I-N-A. Not Teenie.

I'll win because I'm the most enchanting one here!

That what I said. Teenie.

I pick you, Blonde Violet.

Leggings

What?!

Okay, Other Violet. You're with me.

What?!

What?!

Helmet
Mob Head
Elytra
Leggings

help you glide to victory?

Good teams. A little confusing, but we see what happens. Okay, follow rules on board. First team to finish enchanting everything wins.

Leggings

Why is Orange Violet on our team?

I can't tell you. But you have to trust me when I tell you we'll win for sure.

whisper whisper

She's besties with Tina and they all hate us. She'll ruin it for us for sure. Tina is probably making a game plan right now.

I can't tell you why. I was sworn to secrecy.

But I CAN show you. Wait here.

Hey, Violet? Can you please go collect some books for the next challenge?

Not everyone will love this next challenge, but I know you'll all do your best.

The challenge is to craft something spectacular to debut at our school celebration. It's our first ever community celebration project. There are no teams in this one, so it's every student for him or herself.

Yes!

Oh, no!

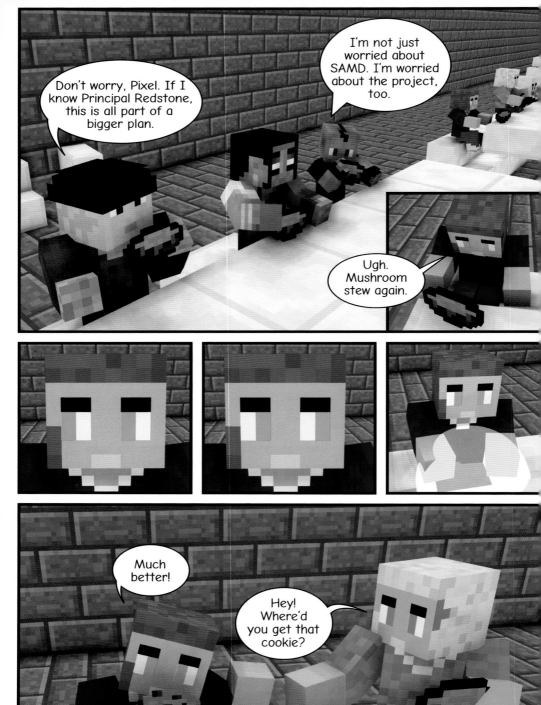

How did you find out?

You told her!

I already knew.

I always carry a few potions with me. I saw you whispering with Tina before the enchanting competition. I wasn't sure we could trust you. I drank an invisibility potion and kind of spied on you.

There was a flash of light, and suddenly a stack of books appeared.

La la la. Building something awesome. Oh yeah. Not sure what it's gonna be.

Does he know?

Yes. I'm sorry. I told Uma and Sky right away. I was kind of freaked out.

Don't worry. They both promise to keep it a secret.

I'm kind of relieved. It's nice not to feel so alone. You guys are much better friends to me than Tina ever was. Or the other Violet, for that matter.

Friends?

Friends!

CHAPTER 6

DOWN IN
THE DARK

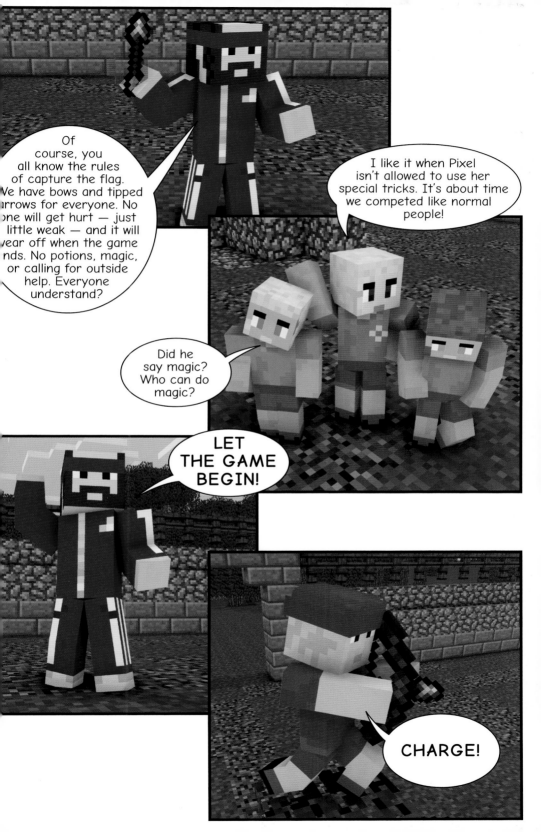

Do you really think Violet is on our side?

I hope she isn't reporting everything back to Tina and double-crossing us. But I guess we really don't have anything to lose.

Speaking of losing, we are about to...

Well that was no fun!

We lost, but we had fun playing. We probably should have done more battling and less talking!

I'm off to change. I think my clothes must be clean by now.

I'll be happy to get out of uniform!

CHAPTER 7

BUILDING
PLANS

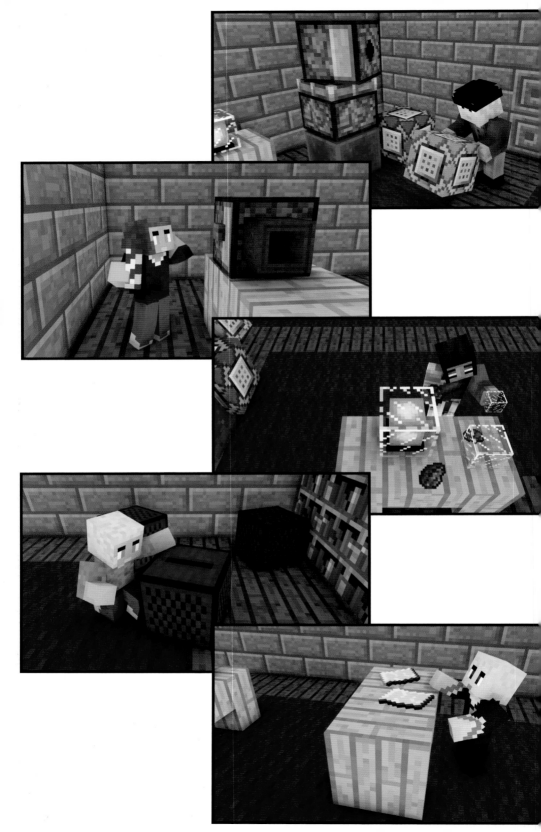

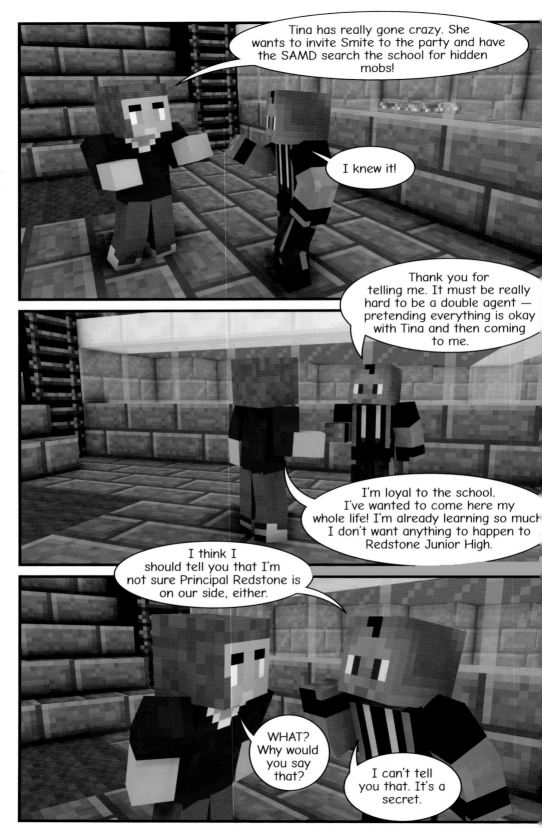

Well, Tina suspects the Principal is hiding mobs in the school. That's crazy, right?

Um, yeah. Totally.

Hey, listen. I'm glad you stopped by, but I'm way behind on my mob homework. Thanks for telling me about Tina's plan. I'll talk to you later, okay?

Okay. Bye.

We have an emergency! Tina's going to invite Smite to the party! She wants the SAMD to win!

What's up, Pixel?

Hello?

That *is* an emergency. We have to tell the principal.

Meet me outside in the field. We have to talk in person.

What are we doing out here?

We needed some privacy.

So you picked a wide-open field?

Tina thinks I have no talents, but I learned a lot growing up on the farm! Planting sugar cane can turn a wide-open field into a private office!

Now we can talk. I wanted to be sure we were completely alone before I told you my plan.

Tina thinks she's going to catch us hiding mobs in the school, so why don't we give her what she expects?

You mean invite the mobs to the party?

That actually makes sense. We already have the creepers and Mr. Z hiding out here.

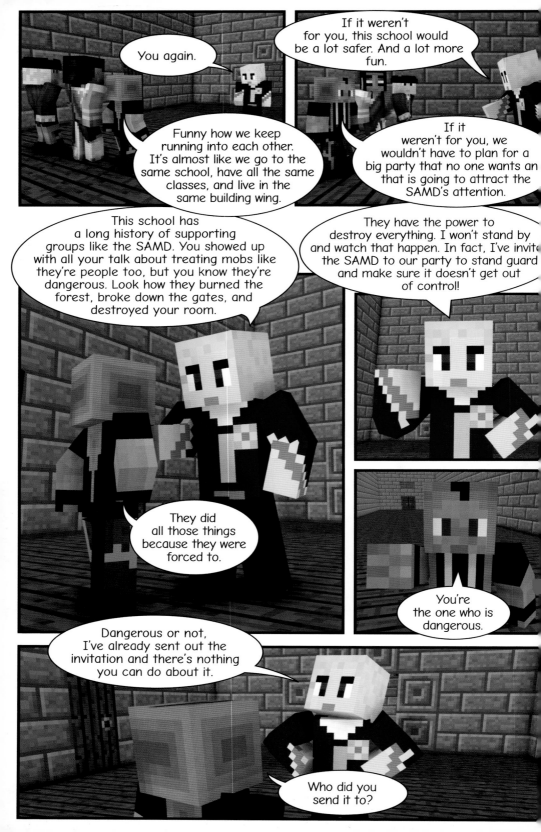

CHAPTER 8

Dust

PARKLE!

Re

Food Milk

Cake Plates

Watermelon Apples Co

r plates

THE PARTY

FAIRIES

Oh! Hello Elliana!

Mooooo.

Good! You're all here. Thank you for coming.

MOOO

BAAA

I wonder what Pixel's big project is. She is using an awful lot of animals. I hope she is putting on a circus. I do love a good show!

Quickly and quietly, now. This way!

Moo?

Really, Elliana. You should have gone before you left home. Go back outside if you have to. We'll wait for you here.

Hey, Pixel. What are you up to?

What ARE you up to? You're nervous. And you're hiding something.

Nothing at all. Just checking on the creepers.

CHAPTER 9

THE MAIN
EVENT

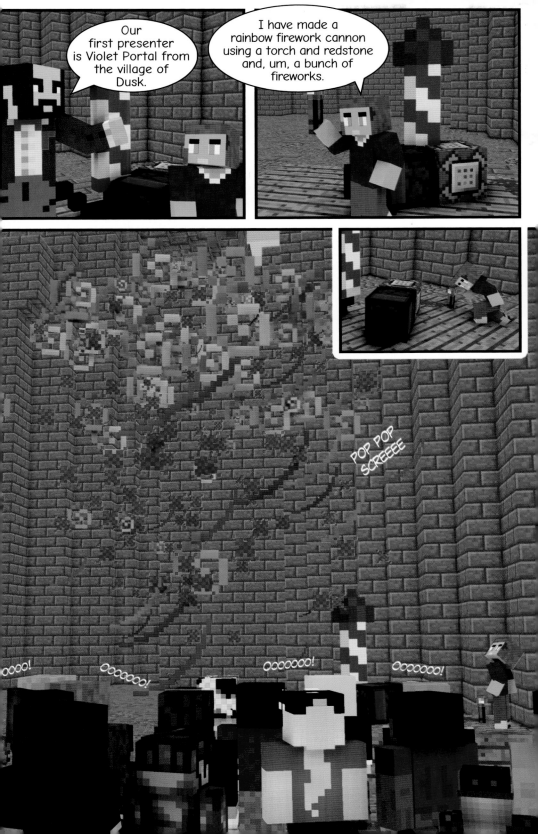

Our next presenter is Sky Torrance, a redstone genius from my own hometown of Terrabyte.

I have created a fireworks show that is timed to look like a wave of light. Each firework also releases a note block, so the result is fireworks set to music.

Our next student comes all the way from the city of Sand. Please welcome Uma Ghosh!

I have created a healing beacon as a welcome to all who come here. My hope is that as you pass through the rays, you will feel peaceful and happy.

I FEEL GREAT!

WOW!

FANTASTIC!

Trap horses!

This too scary for me. Need to hide.

Run!

CHAPTER 10

PARTY CRASHERS

Hisssss. Sssstay away from our massssster!

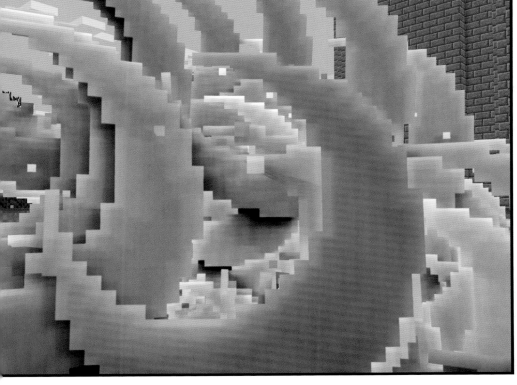

FLIP

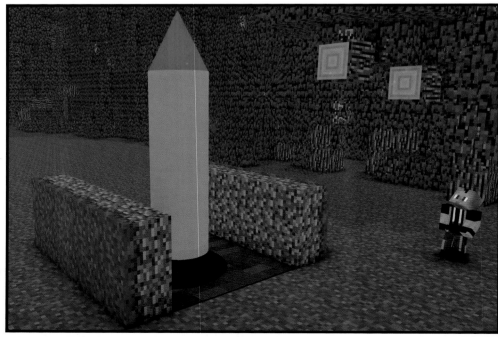

CHAPTER 11

PARTY TIME

CHAPTER 12

HOMECOMING

A fishing pole will... yes Tina?

I was just wondering who won the big orb challenge. You know, the one we had before Pixel almost destroyed the school with those creepers?

It wasn't Pixel who invited the creepers, it was...

What?

Yes, it was me. I did it. No one else. Especially not the principal or any of my friends.

If you remember, Teenie, you got only one orb. Sky won with most orbs. He has most experience now.

Oh yeah! I win 6th grade.

Parkour for the win!

Oops.

AN UNOFFICIAL GRAPHIC NOVEL
FOR MINECRAFTERS

REDSTONE JUNIOR HIGH

DRAGONS NEVER DIE

CARA J. STEVENS

ART BY WALKER MELBY

SKY PONY PRESS
NEW YORK

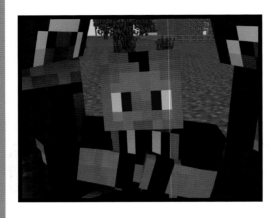

PIXEL: A girl with an unusual way with animals and other creatures.

SKY: A redstone expert who is also one of Pixel's best friends at school.

UMA: A fellow student at Redstone Junior High who can sense how people and mobs are feeling.

CHARACTERS

MR. Z: A teacher with a dark past.

PRINCIPAL REDSTONE:
The head of Redstone Junior High.

SMITE: An evil villian with a ninja army who does everything he can to disrupt the realm.

GALI & OMOL GHOSH:
Uma's worldly and adventurous parents.

INTRODUCTION

When Uma shows up at Pixel's house over summer break, it's not just for a friendly visit. It's to bring chilling news of the Ender Dragon's death. Never before has their world suffered such a great loss. Uma now holds the one item that the Ender Dragon left behind and both girls must protect it with their lives.

The girls return to Redstone Junior High with a sense of purpose and a secret much bigger than the both of them. But what used to be a safe haven for students has been ravaged by the Ender Dragon's destroyer, Smite, and his evil cohorts. Not only has the school been turned upside down, but it's also overrun with mobs seeking protection from a wave of attacks on their homes. Pixel, Sky, Uma, Principal Redstone, and the other students must teach these mobs to fight back for their homes before Redstone Junior High becomes a battlefield and the Ender Dragon's legacy is lost forever.

Will the Ender Dragon finally be avenged or will Smite and his crew wipe out every last ounce of hope for a return to peace and normalcy?

CHAPTER 1

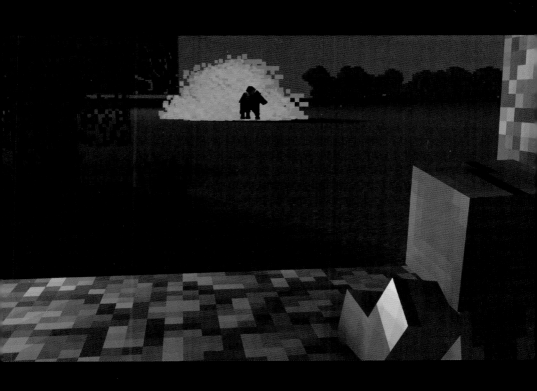

THE SECRET

Pixel's stories are impossible to resist.

...no one at the school suspected that Mr. Z, their favorite teacher, was really the -zombified Rob Zombie — the zombie who started the whole takeover of the school.

I don't know what Tina and the other kids would do if they found out Mr. Z is the zombie who ate her homework at the beginning of the year! Ha ha ha ha!

Ha. The joke's on Tina. She deserves whatever she gets!

Do you think Tina is just misunderstood?

Misunderstood? If she doesn't like Pixel, then she's no friend of mine!

Yeah! That's right!

I'm so lucky to have you guys as my brothers and sisters!

We're lucky to have you, too.

Even if you aren't a great farmer.

MOO!

OINK!

BAA!

Children, lunchtime!

You look different somehow, little sister.

I guess I'm just happy!

I'm so happy to see you!

It's been a long summer away from Redstone Junior High. I have so much to tell you!

What's that?

Shhhh.

Is there somewhere we can go to talk in private?

Follow me.

You know there are spiders following us, right?

Don't worry. They're just spiders.

The ninjas took us by surprise.

We have to follow them. They have all our supplies.

The hav you swor

That's Smite! He's going to destroy her!

Keep still. If they discover us, he will destroy us, too.

You know that guy?

It's a long story, but yes. He is a really bad dude.

He destroyed the dragon, didn't he?

Yes. He used my father's enchanted diamond sword.

I think I felt it earlier. It was like a light went out.

Smite ordered his ninjas to collect as many orbs as they could. He brewed them into a potion, and drank it, restoring his health.

Leave the rest behind. We have enough. We must go.

We can get a lot of gold for this orb.

Grab anything else of ours that you can find!

I know this wasn't mine to take, but I had to save it and I wasn't sure my parents would agree.

You did the right thing, Uma.

The thing is, I don't know anything about dragon eggs. Do you?

Nothing at all!

CHAPTER 2

THE JOURNEY

Thank you for breakfast, Mr. and Mrs. Dot.

Yes, thanks!

Oh don't worry about that, dear. You're leaving for school today. Go have fun.

I can take you to meet my animal friends after we help clean up.

I'm not great at farm chores, so I do the dishes.

That must take all day! I'm an only child. My parents work so much, we usually just eat standing up over the automatic pork chop cooker. I'm not sure we own plates, come to think of it.

I'll miss you, too, Lola. I'm sorry I can't take you with me. I se enough trouble at school hout having to explain why I showed up with a barn-load of animals.

I can sense that your animal friends are very happy here. But they are sad that you are leaving.

That's what I figured. I envy your ability to sense emotions.

Do you think this sheep would mind if I borrowed some wool? The ninjas ripp[ed] my blanket when the[y] stole it from our campsite.

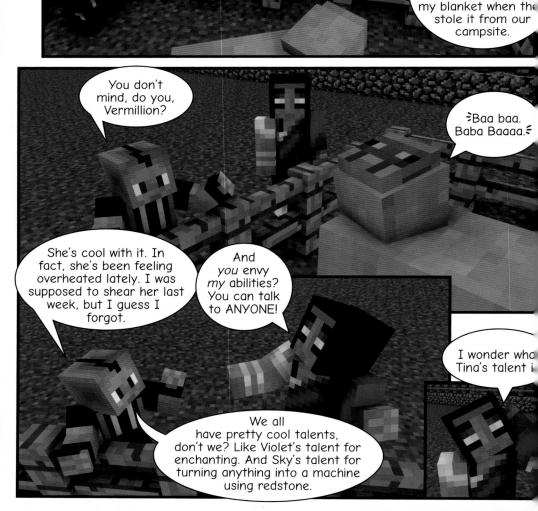

You don't mind, do you, Vermillion?

⸘Baa baa. Baba Baaaa.⸘

She's cool with it. In fact, she's been feeling overheated lately. I was supposed to shear her last week, but I guess I forgot.

And *you* envy *my* abilities? You can talk to ANYONE!

I wonder wha[t] Tina's talent i[s]

We all have pretty cool talents, don't we? Like Violet's talent for enchanting. And Sky's talent for turning anything into a machine using redstone.

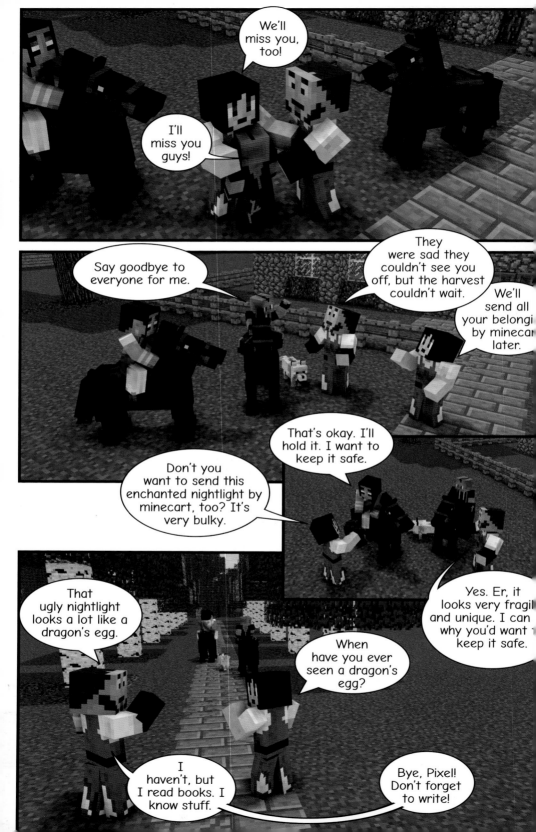

Normally I'd feel nervous traveling through a dark forest with all these spiders following us. But I sense that the spiders are feeling peaceful. They seem to be watching over you, Pixel.

Hi there! Have a nice day!

Clatter! Skrix!

How cute!

Don't you mean "how dangerous?"

They don't want to bother us. They're just having a nice game of tag.

What's wrong, Uma?

Don't look now, but I sense someone — or something — is watching us.

Now I'm weak and defenseless. Look at me! I'm... FLESHY.

Oh!

We had no idea...

Change me back! NOW!

I'm so sorry. We just assumed everyone who was a zombie wanted to be changed back.

That's crazy. Everyone knows that zombies have all the power. We are strong. We travel by night. We are invincible.

You can't open an iron door.

Everyone has their weaknesses.

So will you change me back, or will I have to shoot you?

WOULD YOU PLEASE STOP POINTING THAT THING AT US?

Someone is going to get hurt!

CHAPTER 3

HATCHING
A PLAN

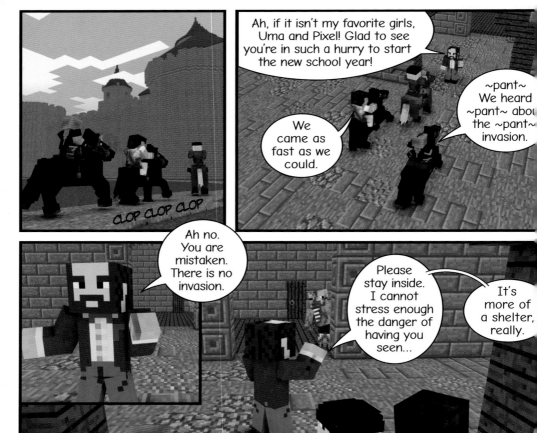

Ah, if it isn't my favorite girls, Uma and Pixel! Glad to see you're in such a hurry to start the new school year!

~pant~ We heard ~pant~ abou the ~pant~ invasion.

We came as fast as we could.

Ah no. You are mistaken. There is no invasion.

Please stay inside. I cannot stress enough the danger of having you seen...

It's more of a shelter, really.

CLOP CLOP CLOP

Last night, Smite and his ninjas tore through the realm, interrogating everyone they met. They are looking for something and won't stop until they find it.

So you took in half the beings in the realm? Are they sleeping in our beds?

OH!

No, of course not. We gave them a hall. Everyone living on the West Wing is to bunk up with someone else. That's a small price to pay to help out our poor defenseless friends.

RATTLE

I didn't think things here could get any stranger than they already were.

Waaahhhhh!

These mobs aren't as defenseless as you think. In fact, a former zombie just shot at me this morning.

I agree. I'm all for protecting everyone, but this is out of control.

See? Nothing scary here. When you learn how to behave yourselves, we will let you out, and then you can have the run of the school.

I did not tell her to say that.

How are you going to get out of there?

I didn't think that part through.

Principal Redstone will be sure to get you everythin you need. I'll be back aft class to check in on you.

I have just enough time to see my room before heading to class.

Oh. About your room. There's something I forgot to tell you.

CHAPTER 4

CHICKENS AND
FRAIDY CATS

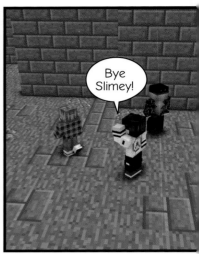

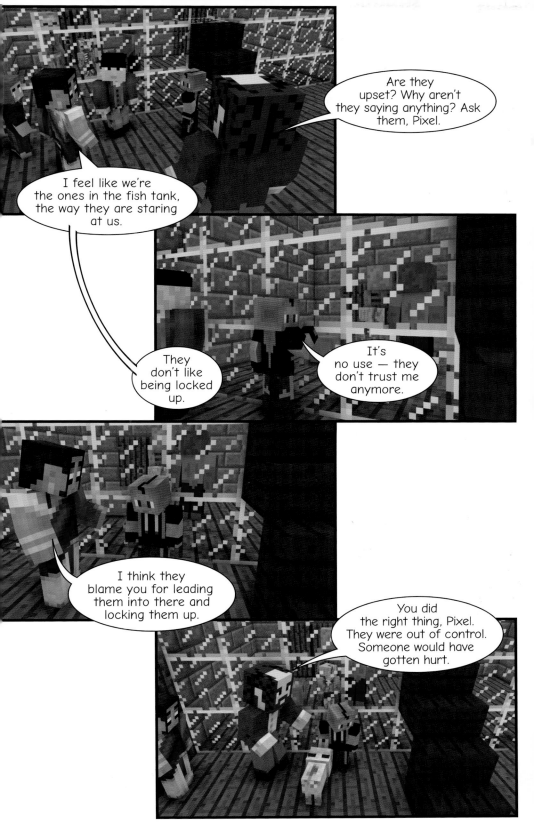

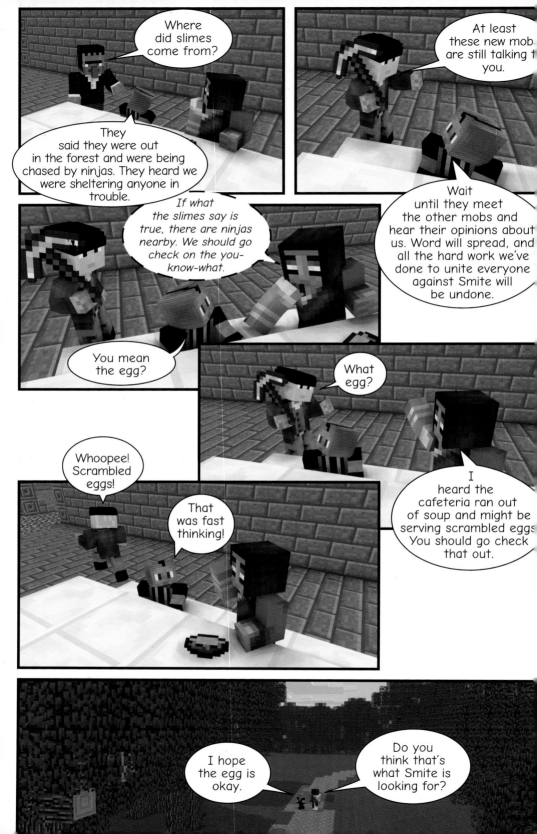

CHAPTER 5

FRIGHT SCHOOL

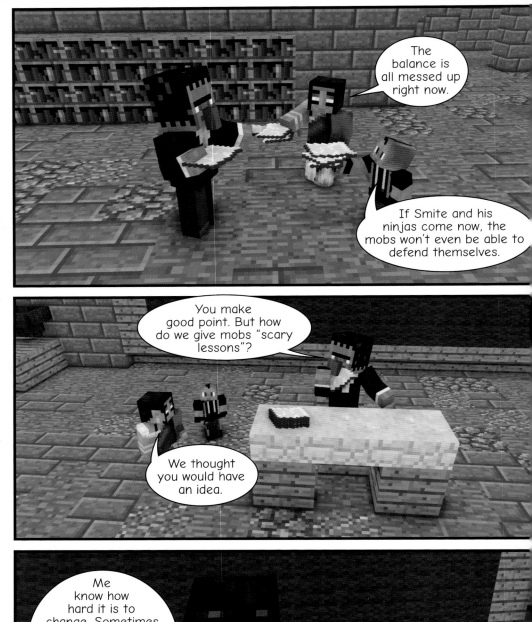

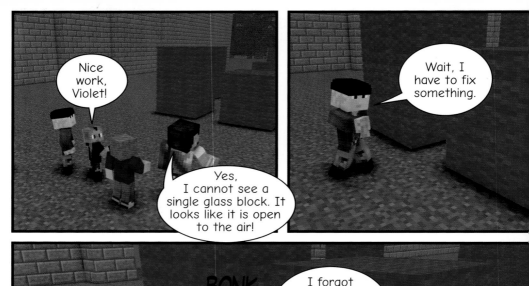

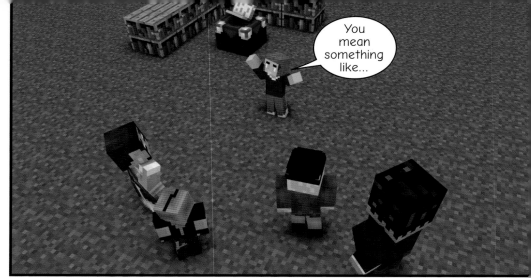

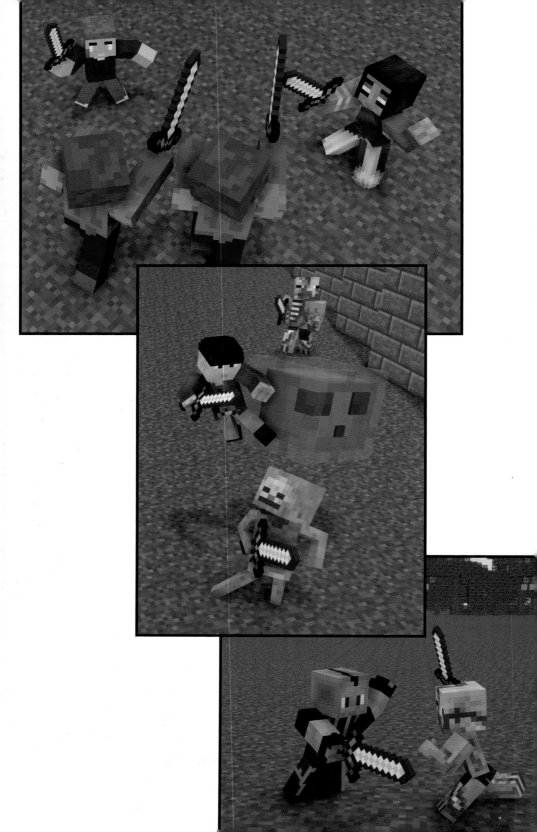

CHAPTER 6

BREAKING THROUGH WALLS

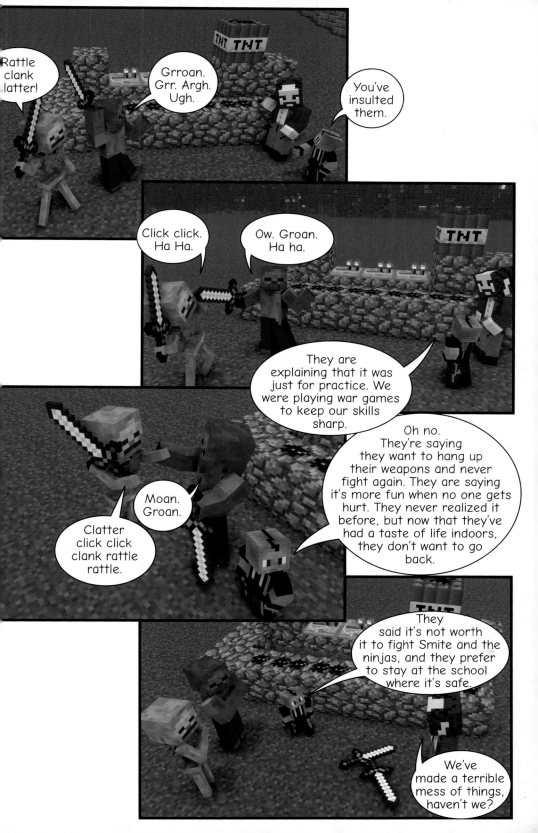

Stand back!

I knew it wasn't an enchanted night light.

What is an enchanted night light?

No clue. Mor important what's this

It's a dragon egg.

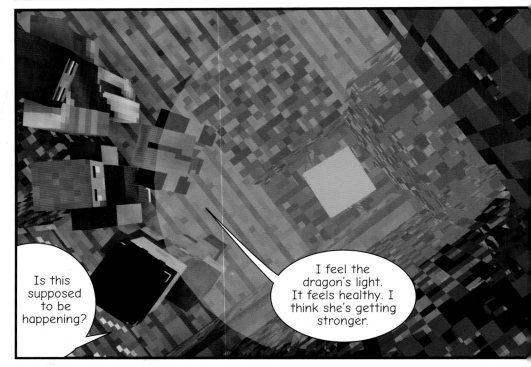

Is this supposed to be happening?

I feel the dragon's light. It feels healthy. I think she's getting stronger.

Long live the new queen!

We forgive you, Pixel Dot. We will protect baby dragon no matter what. Even if it costs us our lives. The Ender Dragon Queen's death will be avenged.

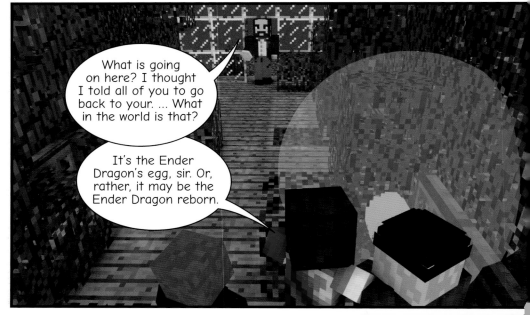

What is going on here? I thought I told all of you to go back to your. ... What in the world is that?

It's the Ender Dragon's egg, sir. Or, rather, it may be the Ender Dragon reborn.

ait, back up. How o you know Sky's mom?

We're not really allowed to say.

It's okay. You can tell her. She has proven she can be trusted. They all can.

We aren't exactly traders working for a multinational company.

We work for Ambassador Prime as secret agents. We track down criminals and watch for illegal trading activity. We didn't expect to run into Smite and his men when we were out with you last week. You weren't supposed to see that awful battle.

I had no idea!

I'm sorry I took the egg without telling you.

It's a good thing you did. The ninjas came back and searched our campsite after you left. They made a big mess of things, but they didn't find the egg. You saved us and the egg!

CHAPTER 7

A COMMON ENEMY

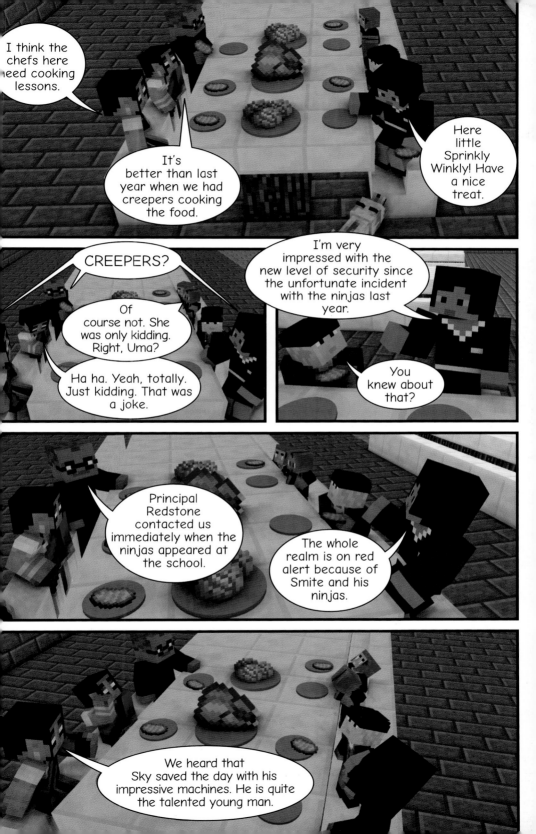

Smite has just been spotted in the Zeta Quadrant. He is tacking an underwater fortress. I have to go.

We'll come with you. We have worked with the Elder Guardians there in the past. They trust us.

You guys are, like, secret agents! I can't believe I never realized how cool you are!

You are pretty cool yourself, young lady. Things are really going to change between us now that we aren't hiding things from each other anymore.

Any other secrets you want to share before we leave?

Nope!

Goodbye, Mom. Be careful!

Don't forget to eat your :ggies, Sky! And take care of hat cute little puppy wuppy, Sprinkles!

Parents can be so embarrassing sometimes.

Not mine. My parents are the coolest!

CHAPTER 8

TEAM
BUILDING

Pixel! Pixel Dot! There you are. I need to speak with you.

I have made a big mistake letting the mobs stay here. I have gotten soft in my old age.

I can't help but feel like it's my fault, too. Ever since I got here, it's been one invasion after another.

The school was mob-free for 100 years before I came.

I am the one who invited them into the school.

I had heard of your extraordinary abilities and visited your house to see for myself.

It's working! They're leaving the school.

I guess music really does calm any savage beast.

Do you like the music?

≒Clatter≒

≒Rattle≒

≒Grunt≒

Yes yes!

CHAPTER 9

EGG-TASTROPHE!

The next morning.

≥yawn≥

Good morning, roommate!

Shhh! Don't wake Violet.

oops. Good morning!

I had such a great night's sleep. Didn't you?

I always sleep so much better here.

It's still pretty early. Do you think we have time to check on Eggie?

You are supposed to be guarding the door.

You are not to touch the egg again without my permission. We don't know how that potion affect the dragon inside.

We're sorry.

Does anyone have the dragon book handy? I think we need to give it a good read before anyone else gets a crazy idea like that.

I borrowed Ambassador Prime's copy.

Fascinating.

What does it say?

Is that the book about caring for a dragon egg?

Created in the heart of a star, the Dragon Queen rules the End with her thought and her inner power. She lives out her life in a vast void. No day or night. No time or direction. Her only company is the four pillars that surround her throne and the crystals that light her way. In this void, she protects untold secrets. She loves every creature in creation, even those who come to challenge her. When warriors come, the Queen welcomes the challenge, for in challenge comes company and a break from the endless, timeless loneliness.

Once the Dragon Queen has been defeated, she will drop the experience she has gathered over her lifetime and her remaining energy will be transferred to an egg. There, she will grow strong again, pulling new energy from the sun and moon and all the beauty of the world she has never seen.

Once she has been vanquished, she will drop into a deep, restful sleep. Deep in the dream of a game, the dragon will dream of the world she has never seen: light, trees, snow, sand, water, and creatures full of light and love. She will dream of hunting and being hunted. And she will grow stronger. This process will take time and should never be tampered with in any way or the Queen may suffer great harm.

Care of the dragon's energy egg is a delicate matter, and should only be handled by an expert.

If you find the egg, do not touch or move the shell. Contact the Department of Dragon Studies immediately.

Does it say anything about how to hatch it?

How do we contact the Department?

We don't. That is the first place Smite will look for it.

So that's why Uma's parents said we should keep the egg here. Who would suspect that a bunch of kids would be trusted with the most important artifact in the universe?

CHAPTER 10

NINJAS!

That's what we get for saving the world.

Secret agents are always so misunderstood.

Today, me no have friend to share with you. Principal Redstone said we had to let Slimey go.

Slimey gave me hug when he left.

Important note: slime hugs very painful. Do not hug slime. Good lesson for you.

Ninja

Me know this is mob education class, but there is new danger to everyone and we need to study its behavior.

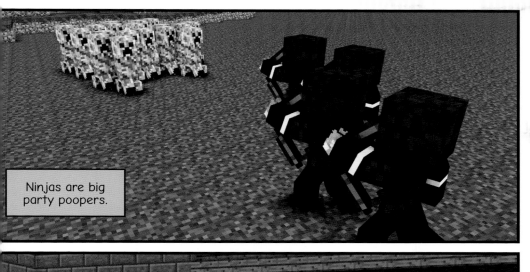

Ninjas are big party poopers.

Some of you not here last year to see when they came in and ruined big party. Ninjas are sneaky, fast, and quiet.

They also like to destroy things.

CHAPTER II

THE BATTLE

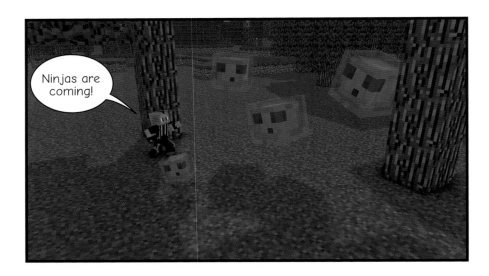

Get some milk and healing potion! Quick!

Where is Sky? And where is Principal Redstone?

Almost finished, Sir! Building an incubator out of nothing is not as easy as it looks.

Did you hear the explosion? Hurry, Sky. We're running out of time!

CHAPTER 12

A QUEEN IS BORN

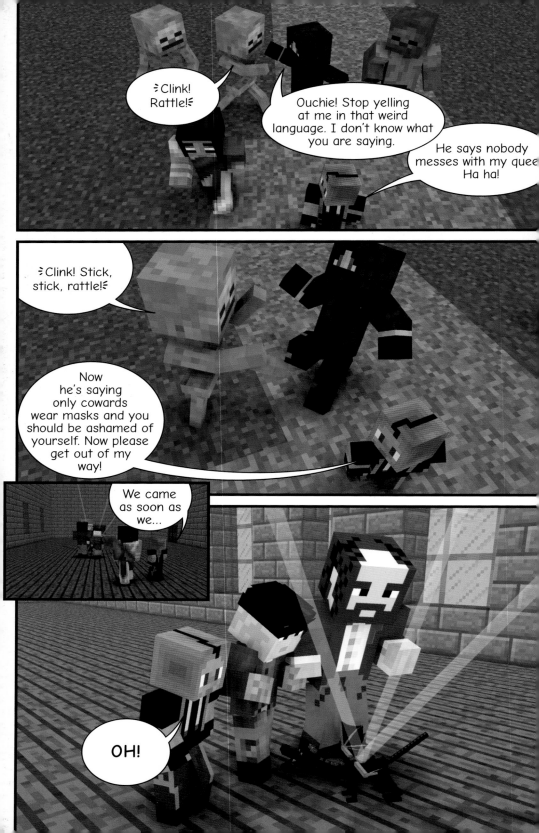

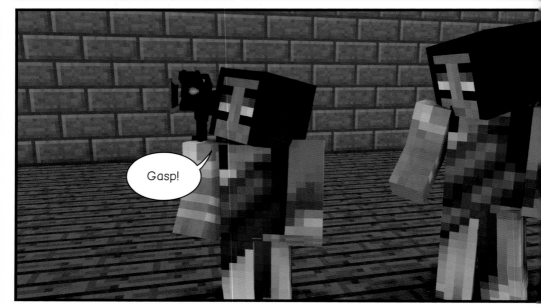

She has chosen you. Lift your hands like this to get her to rise up.

Chosen me?

You rescued her egg. You held the egg close to your heart to protect it. You created the bond.

w the light! he dragon okay?

mbasssador! Wait! The tions haven't en effect yet.

Mom! What happened to you?

After years of planning, we expected we would be the ones to train the new queen.

Uma's special abilities to sense feelings will make her an even better trainer. And we will be by her side the whole time.

he is autiful!

Smite knocked the Ambassador down. She needs to rest.

The fighting continues. We must support our allies. They need our help.

The dragon can help, but we need more time.

She is still just a baby.

⹀Hic⹀

Awwwww!

She has the hiccups!

⹀sniff, sniff⹀

⹀hiccup⹀

⹀hic⹀

⹀YIPE!⹀

Ninjas! Get that dragon!

=Skreeee!=

Poor baby.

That baby just defended herself with a hiccup!

Up! Rise up!

=Skrixxx=

We need the strength of a fully-grown dragon. It will take weeks for her to grow big and strong.

We don't have weeks. We don't even have minutes. Smite will be back with more ninjas soon.

s may help. And we can get her ear a beacon, I k we can give her emporary boost at will last just g enough for a ood battle.

And afterward she will go back to being a baby? So she can be trained properly?

Yes, sir.

We're ready for you, Violet. Let's get enchanting!

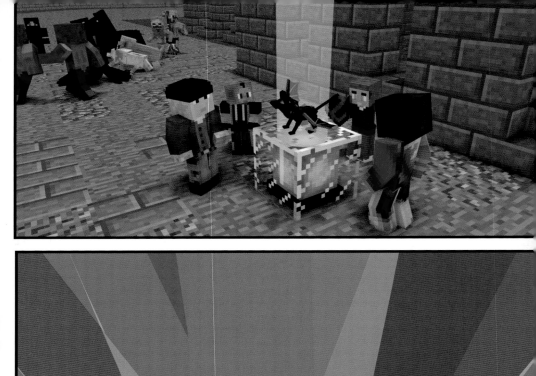

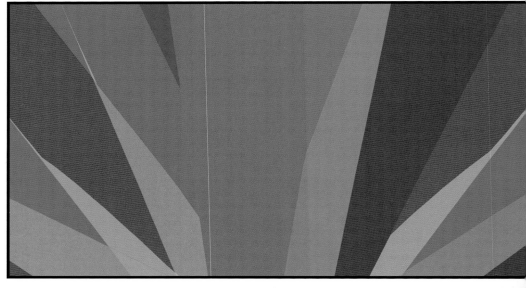

CHAPTER 13

THE QUEEN'S GUARD

Bye, Sky. Love you to pieces.

Goodbye, Uma dear. Goodbye, Dragon Queen!

Bye, Mom!

Bye, Mom and Dad!

I can't believe we defeated Smite once and for all!

I'm glad our parents were here to help. And I'm glad the cat is out of the bag about my special abilities.

Are you confused, Sprinkles? I'm sensing confusion coming from you.

I think Sprinkles w curious about cat in the b

Letting the cat out of the bag is an expression that means sharing a secret. There are no cats involved here.

That's strange. I've never been able to read Sprinkles' emotions before.

We have enough friends in the forest to call on if we need help. I think your golem-making days are over, Sky.

Maybe you've finally found the one thing you can't make.

You can't blame a guy for trying.

The stakes are too high for you to try again. The last one almost got us all destroyed—the dragon, too!

≋Skrixx!≋

≋Cluuuuuck!≋

BONK!

THUD!

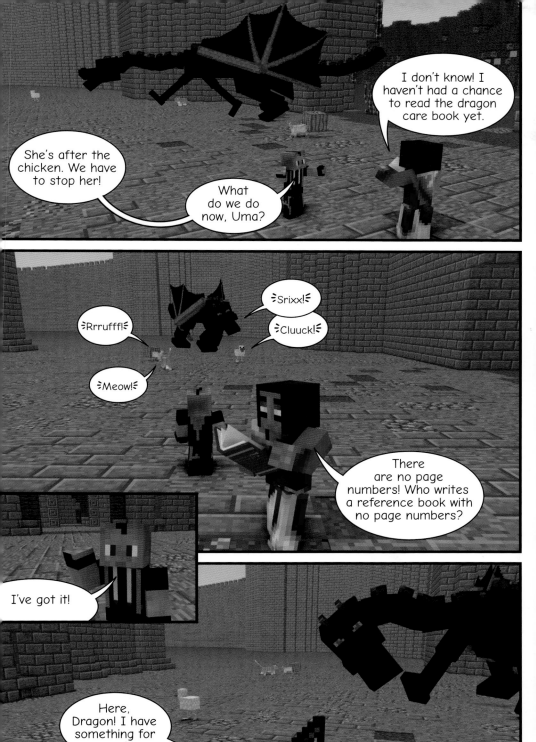

I guess she likes carrots. Nice job, Pixel.

Hey Sky, we are going to need a way to keep our little dragon friend safe and out of trouble.

I'm way ahead of you, friend!

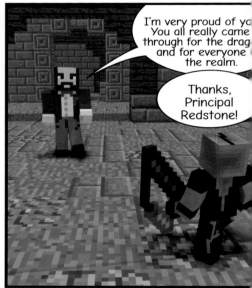

I'm very proud of yo You all really came through for the drag and for everyone the realm.

Thanks, Principal Redstone!

I'm sorry we made such a mess of the school again.

That's all right, Uma. It all turned out for the best.

I have a big favor to ask of you. It's about the dragon.

I have a few ideas for how to make her stay here more comfortable for everyone, if you'd like to see them.

If you're going to ask if we can keep the dragon at the school while you train her, the answer is yes. Mr. Z and I are making arrangements for her to stay in the West Wing.

I would. As long as it doesn't involve creating anoth golem with artificial intelligence.

One week later...

Today, we have new special guest in Mob Education: Dragon Queen.

This is a lot more exciting than learning about slimes!

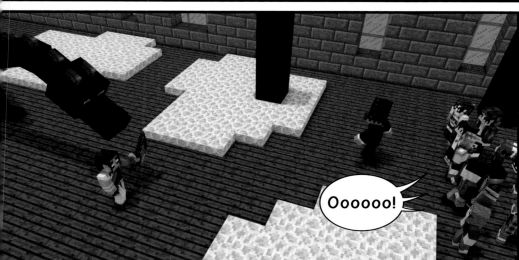

Oooooo!

Huh?

Gasp!

Noooo!

Bad dragon!

That's better. Good girl!

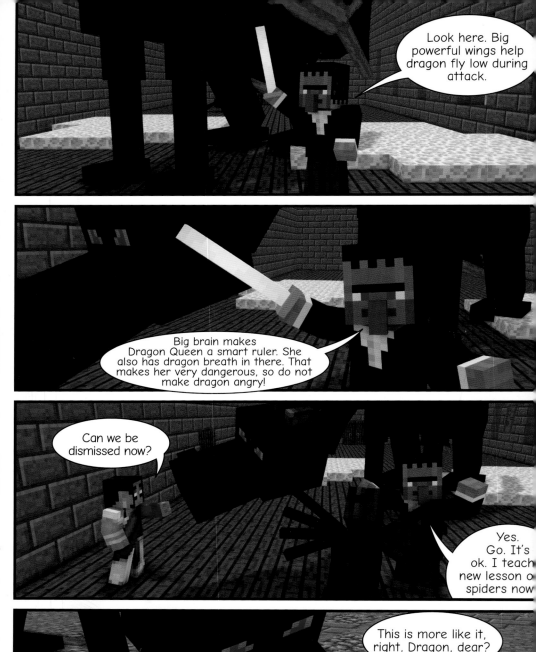